ADVENTURES IN MARTYRDOM

ADVENTURES IN MARTYRDOM

Krissie Williams

SMALL DOGMA PUBLISHING
LAKELAND, FLORIDA

Small Dogma Publishing
Lakeland, Florida 33804

Printed in the United States of America on acid free paper.

Cover Design by Small Dogma Publishing, Inc.

ISBN 978-1-935267-03-4

LCCN 2009927082

13 12 11 10 09 10 9 8 7 6 5 4 3 2

Congratulations! You are a LifeSaver!

Literally... by buying this book, you most likely saved a life. Small Dogma Publishing has committed to donate 50 cents from each book sale to the Feed The Children Campaign dedicated to end world hunger and poverty. Right now, a person dies every three seconds from starvation or poverty related illness... most likely a child under the age of 5. This child's death could have been prevented by pennies worth of food and medication.

What a tragedy it is that something so preventable is happening in such record numbers. And while 50 cents per book isn't much, it is something, and if we can all individually just do something, we can make a huge difference as a whole. If you would like to know more about ending hunger please visit www.feedthechildren.org or look for their link on www.smalldogma.com. Again, thank you for your support and enjoy your purchase.

Sincerely,

Matt Porricelli, M.B.A.
President
Small Dogma Publishing

Contents

1

Broken Window

Today's the day! That's it. I am three pills away from ending it all. I'm gonna do it. It's too much bullshit. Too much insignificant and significant bullshit. Where are my pills and chardonnay? A nice little cocktail. That'll work.

I glanced at the clock. 10:14 am. I had better enjoy these last three days of freedom. Work is only 72 hours away. What a hot mess. My morning fuzz time was going to get short again. Aren't those the best moments? The ones when you just wake up, hanging in dream and reality with a little fuzz. The mind hasn't kicked in yet, but you are aware that you are transitioning into the world. Then, about a minute and fifteen seconds later, it hits you. The problem from yesterday. The fight that you had with your boyfriend the night before. The evaluation from the boss. The realization that the relationship is dust. What you have to take care of today. Or simply the fact that your bladder is calling and you had better hurry up and tap the ground surface to keep from having an accident.

For me, after emerging from the transition state, it is recalling the brief encounter I had at my doctor's office the day before. At about noon, there was a message on my machine.

"Hi Kara, this is Dr. Conroy's office. We were wondering if you could call us back and schedule an appointment to go over the results of your pap. Thanks."

Holy Shit. What the hell does that mean? I had better make this my priority this afternoon. Luckily, the office is only about fifteen minutes away and they take walk-ins, so I figure it is just easier to stop by on my way to the dreaded gym.

I arrived, signed in, told the receptionist about my message, and slunk into a chair. Staring at the amount of elderly women in the waiting room forced me to contemplate my own mortality. What was this about? I usually had paps that were fine. Most gynecologists generally have the policy that if they don't contact you after your exam, if there isn't a problem. Well, that's not the case with me, is it? It never is. There is a problem.

Have you ever seen those commercials that just rattle off a bunch of statistics? "2 out of 3 people lose weight with our product. Act Fast." Or "Virtually everyone is guaranteed approval. Apply NOW!" It seems as though I am always the third person who doesn't lose the weight, or the one who doesn't get approved. After a while, you just get used to it. You begin to subconsciously accept that your lot in life is just a little bit harder than everyone else's. Now don't get me wrong, things could be much worse all around. But a cervical cancer scare at age 33 isn't fun either.

Yep- that's right. Dr. Conroy is referring me to a reputable gynecologist for a biopsy. I have never had one, and I am absolutely terrified. So I am going to lie in this bed for another half hour or so and pretend that this is not happening right now. Not happening, considering the fact that in three days I have to go back to school and teach. Not happening considering that approximately a week ago, my boyfriend called me and told me he wanted to be friends.

Total abandonment by him. *Not happening.* If I squeeze my eyes really hard and clap my ears this will all go away. But it doesn't. Instead, it just creeps along, like a quiet train arriving at a station at midnight. Breaking it to my parents is the easy part. After brief shock and disbelief, my mother immediately transferred into caregiver and deaconess. I knew she had my back. Minutes later, dad called from work, enthusiastically stating that he is praying for me. One thing I will say about black folks in the church, they will pray for you even at your Judgment Day with the man upstairs. The devil could be carting you off, with God standing in tow after making his decision, and there will be a church lady, wearing a pink hat with a poufy yellow flower holding a Bible screaming. "Devil don't take her! Be loosed child!" The pink hat lady was probably the dead spirit of some preacher's wife. Church people take crises seriously. Sometimes I wish I had faith like that, minus the dogma.

I have learned that once you encounter the possibility that you may be sick, the waiting that is the worst part. The not knowing. Faking to keep your mind off things, keeping busy with inane tasks and watching crappy comedies on

TV. Except for *Family Guy*, that is a funny ass show. And it's not like I don't have a million things to do. It's just that, after another summer of doing nothing, who wants to do something at the end? Just to convince yourself that you were somewhat productive for the last 10 weeks? Lately, I didn't even have enough energy to even bullshit myself anymore. I'll leave that to the random men and friends that pushed their way into my existence. But that's another story.

The next day, I find enough energy to clean my apartment. It isn't bad. It isn't great. Its home. I contemplate something my doctor said to me at the visit. "The good news is that if you do have it, cervical cancer is probably the only cancer that is 100% curable."

Well, gee, isn't that comforting? What they didn't tell me is that any type of cancer could always come back. Of course I know that, but funny how my doctor conveniently withheld that information. Deep down, I know it could be worse, and I am thankful for my blessings, but I still can't help being angry at the universe, God, and the whole lot of angels up there. Everybody says when something bad happens, pray it through. Well, I'm officially on a prayer strike. I want my meds to be my divine intervention.

Okay, so enough wallowing, one day of summer vacation left. I quickly decide that I am going to deal with the world today, try to laugh a little and pretend I was someone else. Perhaps I'll go to the beach with Brittany. She was my road dog. Aaargh- the thought of wearing a bathing suit makes me nauseous. But besides Florida and California, I pretty much am living in the beach capital of the nation, Cape Cod, Massachusetts. I stand in the middle of my tiny bedroom staring into the antique mirror I had received from my mom when my grandmother passed away. I was about 5ft. tall with milk chocolate skin, like the color of a Reese cup on the outside. I was average weight, what was that these days for women anyway? I guess about a size 12 or 14 depending on the time of the month. Would love to be a size 8 or 10. Forever trying to lose that last 10 pounds. *Forever.* Ample boobs. Big boobs, but not Playboy size boobs. And they are real. I'm sure the feminists will be pissed off at me for referring to my breasts as boobs. So for all of you feminists out there- breasts. Oh and I have a short haircut. Sometimes I want to grow it long, but then I quit after a few months. Too much work. It's all about minimal effort. I can be stylish when I need to but a lot more days it seems that I am frumpy. That's probably why I don't have a man.

Oh I have a friend, with "occasional benefits". He's an ex that I continue to share a deep bond with. We often keep finding ourselves back to each other, when life got rough or we break up with someone else. We joke that if we aren't with someone at age 35 then we'll just elope and get it over with. I feel our relationship has a comfortability and an uncomfortability. He knew me inside and out, and yet there were parts of myself I wished to stay hidden that he examined. Why did I still long for something or someone else? He was good to me, and yet at times I believed I had to push for the fairytale ending. Denying that I've outgrown our relationship keeps me secure.

As I step outside my apartment Dawn, my neighbor, is sitting on her step flicking a cigarette.

"Hey", she shouted. "Where are you off to?"

"Good Morning Dawn." I continue my walk to my car, "Going to the beach with Brittany."

"Well, you have fun," she retorts, as if angry that I didn't invite her. "I'll stop by later." I'm sure you will Dawn, you always do.

Dawn is a certified nut. I live next door to someone who could be committed or arrested at the drop of a phone call. I mean, I suffer from depression, but Dawn is crazy. Not all the time, just sporadically. At times the sporadic became more consistent if her life isn't going right. I think she borders on the line of bipolar or something. Still, it is the kind of crazy you love. It can also be the kind of crazy where she sucks you into her world and you start cheering her on for being insane enough to do the things you wish you could do. Sometimes she did suck me in. Emotionally unstable people can be very manipulative. They can be vampires.

The beach is crowded, too many tourists trying to squeeze in the last few hours before school kicked in. I am just like them, trying to squeeze a little happiness in a needle. Constriction all around. As I lay on my towel in my Donna Karan Marshalls $19.99 bathing suit, I watch an old couple playing in the water with their grandkids. Brittany had run off to the food stand and is taking forever to get back with our hamburgers. She offered to pay, so I happily comply to wait in this heat. It is about 90 degrees today. Even the seaside breezes aren't blowing. I closed my eyes. Something with the cancer scare shook me. Don't know why, but I felt it was a premonition to a banner bad year. I measure my years in school years, and this one is off to a hell of a start.

2

Gilded Bubble

C ape Cod. It is about a little over an hour southeast of Boston to be exact, but it often feels like its own entity. That is, except when the Patriots or the Red Sox go to the Super bowl or the World Series. That type of fever spread across the state. Depending on which way you came, you had to cross the Sagamore or Bourne Bridge to be officially "on Cape." And boy do people kill themselves to be on Cape. Especially in the summer. At any one time, there could be up to a million tourists visiting or at least it felt like that. I still don't understand the lure of this place. It measures about 70 miles long and 1000 square miles with about 600 of it coastline. If you want to be even more re-mote, you can catch the ferry from there and hop to the

Vineyard or Nantucket. The region is known as Cape Cod, but it actually is comprised of about 15 towns or so. Hyannis is considered the largest village of the Cape. This is where I teach high school, social studies to be exact.

Many people have a distortion about this place. Let's discuss. Yes, there are parts of the Cape that represent quintessential New England, and you can't beat the salt air to put you in the mood for a great summer nap. I'm sure you have probably heard "The Kennedys" have a residence here. They are a part of our local history: they have and continue to be very good to this community. It is not uncommon to bump into one of them on Main Street every now and then. There are many wealthy class people who own vacation homes here, including my parents. It is a nice escape for a family vacation. There are parts of the Cape where you truly feel like this is God's country. The beauty of the land is unscathed. There was a full lunar eclipse a few months ago, and I don't believe I could have watched it from a more beautiful place. It is moments like that when I enjoyed living here. I enjoy the quiet. One of my friends has a house a few feet from the Hyannis docks. I love to watch the boats come in at sunset. I all but spring into action when she calls me for an invitation to a barbeque.

But there is another Cape Cod. The truth of the matter is this little island had big city problems. (Is it an island or peninsula? People disagree. After the canal was built, I think they tried to call it an island.) Anyway there are problems. Hyannis, considered the biggest village, is a city. I don't care what anyone says. People are in denial. Anyplace that has an Old Navy and Olive Garden is a city. Now if you have ever been to Martha's Vineyard, it has towns. All you see are mom-pop shops and tiny one-man restaurants for miles. Someone told me a few years ago that Hyannis was ranked among the top ten areas in Massachusetts for homeless. I believe it. Most of the people who do live here year round are middle class, or poor, unless you are a town employee. Even then you could be just blessed enough to have year round full time work. Young professionals who draw decent salaries, such as myself exist but are rare. To be African American doing this is even more mysterious. If you run a business, you had better make a killing during the tourist season because after Columbus

Day your profits are dry. Many businesses actually close for the winter and reopened in March or April.

There is a huge drug problem here that no one wants to talk about. I witness it firsthand at school. I think the drug problem out here is bigger than it is in Boston. Here's my theory. The problem that the Cape faces is one that was faced by other cities in the 1990's. It is almost like they are in the midst of a drug revolution that other places have already gone through and responded to. There are not enough programs for youth and the highlight of their week is getting completely annihilated on a Saturday night. There are also alcoholics who simply drink because they are bored out of their minds in the winter. Then winter becomes spring. Spring becomes summer. Summer becomes fall and, "Will you just please pour me another drink?" You get the point. Drug deals and shootings do occur. Pill popping might as well be listed as an extracurricular activity at my high school. The Cape is not quite as bad as Boston in terms of crime, but I definitely lock my car at night. My car stereo isn't going to get a meth head high. Hell no. It is not that type of party.

And yet I find myself assuming the noble profession of teaching in the midst of this strangeness. I am one of about six people of color on staff. Townshend High School is diverse. Again- another misconception about this place. T High (as most people called it) is about 35% minority these days and growing. We have it all, Black, White, Native American, Brazilian and Asian. It is a typical high school from one glance in the cafeteria. Jocks and preps sit in the middle, the Black table is off to the side, geeks and nerds and other unsociables scattered in between. The students love to tell me about the food fights. I love hearing about them. I only wish the staff echoed the growing diversity of the student population. It is quite difficult to recruit people of color to work out here.

So today is D-Day. The day Barnstable Public Schools snatched my life back for 10 months. I sign in and am handed a badge that states Kara Campbell, Social Studies Teacher, THS written in thick black letters. This was some new shit. Since when did we have to wear badges the first day of school? This is generally a day of meetings with faculty and various departments. I hate badges. I was annoyed already. Our superintendent stood to make her annual speech.

"Good Morning and Welcome Back! Let's get excited for our most successful school year ever!" she cries exuberantly. Oh, good grief. It was only 8:30 in the morning. The teachers surrounding me and I glance at each other in apathy. Does she expect us to catch her enthusiasm like an STD? This crowd isn't being pimped like that. The reality is it is another school year, the old timers were one year closer to retirement and everyone else was counting the days until the next vacation. Cleaning up our classrooms and preparing for new students is the easy part: uncluttering the dysfunctional lives of a number of the students we teach is hard.

At about two-thirty the next morning, my phone is ringing uncontrollably. "Hello," I answer groggily.

"Hey, it's me."

"What the hell do you want, Dawn?" Now I was pissed. The students are coming back tomorrow and I have to be in fit mental shape to deal with America's Future Rejects. And this chick is calling me in the middle of night?

"I got fired today."

She takes a long pause, and then jumps right into the story.

Apparently there was an incident at the restaurant where she worked. There had been a married couple who had been harassing her all summer. They were probably snowbirds. Somehow she always got stuck waiting on them. Tonight was the last straw. I can't quite recall what was said between them, but there were a few bitches and assholes tossed around in the conversation, all capped off with Dawn dumping two Greek salads on the customers' heads. I wanted to laugh and at the same time, kill her for calling me this late. Instead, I keep the conversation short and promise to talk to her after work the next day. I'm not worried about her; drama is Dawn's middle name. Shortly thereafter, I roll over and pop another sleeping pill in my mouth. Aah, my savior.

3

Kismet

My psychiatrist is soooooo wack. I believe he is truly the most boring white man I have ever encountered in my entire life. The only reason why I see him is because I have no choice. I am on maintenance therapy. This means that in order to receive my prescriptions for meds, I have to check in with my psychiatrist a minimum of once a month. I look at the clock in the waiting room. 3:17 pm. Not only was he boring, he was habitually late. He needed to hurry the fuck up. If they don't call me soon, there is going to be a homicide. I'm sure mental patients have killed for less. If it happened I would just say that I was obsessive compulsive and that's what drove me to it. It would happen in a mental health office-what better place to commit a crime? Parent/Teacher night is tonight at the school, and I still need to run home and check the mail and eat a quick bite. Finally, my name is called and I walk into his office.

Dr. Martin's office is the standard puke blue color with a few accolades scattered on the wall. It resembles a sterile generic psychiatrist's office. Just as boring as his personality. When I first met him I couldn't help but notice the ring on his finger. *Holy crap- this man is married?* I said to myself. There had better be someone for me. If he is getting some lifetime ass and I never meet anyone and marry there's going to be hell to pay when I get up there. It would be another thing to add to my long list of complaints for the man upstairs. I can see it now. Everyone else in line is standing there happy they made it to heaven, and there I will be with a pink pad written full of issues that I need to discuss with the Angel Gabriel. If he is busy, any general angel assistant would do. Most definitely the meeting was going to take place before I went to take my place on a cloud.

He had cut his hair since our last meeting. Now his physical features made him resemble even more of a modern day Hitler. The only thing missing is the razor clad moustache.

"Hello Kara, how are you doing today?" he asks in his usual monotone voice. I nod as he pushes away from me and flings around to find my file. "Have there been any significant changes since last month? Hey, you changed your hair color, looks good on you." He adds. I could always count on him to notice my hair. Maybe he has a hair fetish.

"Thanks, and no, no changes, everything is going well. I am back at school and into the swing of things."

"Good, good. Keeping busy helps to keep your mind off negative things." He answers. Keep my mind off what? *The daily internal battle to stop from getting off this merry-go-round and killing myself?* I start to open my mouth and hesitate. I didn't feel like getting into it with him. Here I am in a healing establishment and choosing not to heal. Besides I have no time for discussion today. Time is of the essence.

He summarily writes prescriptions for *Celexa* and *Trazodone* at the appropriate milligrams and bid me goodbye. I stopped by the desk, make my appointment for next month, and get the hell outta there. I live in Falmouth, about a half hour from Hyannis, and I need to beat the small rush hour traffic we did have. In addition, the tourist season is dragging on longer than usual this year. The damn tourists are still causing traffic jams. They need to go the hell home. It is time they accept the reality that the long New England winter was right around the corner.

Later that evening, I am in my classroom trying to straighten up my desk before the parents arrived. My, it got chilly all of a sudden. I don't have any windows open because it is raining outside. Where the hell is that breeze coming from? A grey shadow flies across the room. Diagonally across from me standing next to a globe is an African American woman. She looks about forty-five or fifty. There are a few gray streaks in her long black hair, and she is dressed in one of those dusky dark brown dresses many women wore during the Great Depression. She gives me a melancholic look and presses her finger lightly on the globe. The globe rotated slowly a couple of times.

"Can I help you?" I asked.

She clapped her hands together, quickly pressed one finger to her mouth and whispered "Shhh! Soon you will understand."

Here we go again. Another one of these damn cryptic messages. By the time I had regained my composure she was gone.

Time to go to the bathroom to do one last hair and makeup check. I really need to get my hair cut this weekend. I stare at the mirror, reapply some lip gloss and make a smirk. "Showtime." I say to myself.

I'm not a mother, but as a teacher I can tell you that Parent/Teacher night is a little like the *Westminster Kennel Dog Show*. Parents arrive, sizing the teachers up and categorizing them. It's like you know that you're going to be the subject of the book club discussion the next Saturday. *Maartha, how do you like our son's biology teacher? I noticed her skirt was a little short.* Just to let you parents know we watch you too.

You are placed in different categories yourself. We notice the ones who feel guilty and give their kid the world. There are the ones who want to live vicariously through their child. There are the jock parents. You can't tell them a single thing because *their kid* is going to college on a sports scholarship period. Let's not forget the denial parents. They are the worst to deal with. There are the parents who are mad at the world, including you because they sucked in high school and they believe it is every teacher's mantra in life to fail every kid on their roster. Like we get some extra money in our paychecks for every kid we fail. Yeah, right. And in the incredible shrinking category are the parents who actually give a damn about their child succeeding in life. However, nothing in my nine years of this career can prepare me for the next type of parent I encounter.

I normally teach World History and the majority of my classes are freshmen. I always get a moderately good turnout of parents. Most are a little taken aback at the fact that I'm African-American, but not in a negative sense. They are just used to white teachers interacting with their children. They settle right into the desks and listen intently. Since the schedule rotates to mimic an abbreviated high school day, I usually end up doing this spiel three or four times. I could rattle this crap off in my sleep.

About five minutes into the second speech for the evening I hear my classroom back door creek open. A tall figure comes in quietly and slides into a desk as if not to disturb anyone. I don't look directly in the direction because I am mid-sentence answering a question. I can tell he's black. I am feeling weird all of a sudden. Something is up. I put my game face on. I continue with my introduction, go over the year's curriculum and talked about research assignments. I have my horse blinders on, because I could tell this brother was FINE already just by his demeanor. No peripheral vision required. Besides, I don't want to give myself away. If I glance in his direction I just might faint, get up and drop the panties right there. After finishing my talk, a couple cornered me to ask specifically about how their son is doing in my class. *Whew. I'm out of the woods.* Thank God somebody up there's looking out for a sistah. Now I can somewhat relax and not acknowledge him. The bell rang and the couple still continues to talk to me and then begins to leave.

Oh no, he is still there. Obviously he is hanging around wanting to introduce himself and ask about his kid's grade. I want to scream to the couple walking out "Wait! Help me please don't leave me trapped with this fine Black man! I may do something that I could get arrested for!" But it's too late. He's in my face.

He gives a slight but warm smile and sticks out his hand to shake. "Hi, I'm Evan Warner, Brian's dad."

"Hi, I'm Ms.Campbell, nice to meet you." I flash my pearly whites and shake his hand. I scan his hand quickly. We women are so good at doing this on the sly. No ring. Good sign.

"I just want to let you know that if you ever need to talk to me about Brian, don't hesitate to contact me." I notice he is impeccably dressed in a business casual way. Charcoal gray slacks, pinstripe shirt, burgundy sweater, black shoes. Still, I haven't looked at him directly for a considerable amount of time yet. I can't bring myself to do it. Because I'm vertically challenged (short) I just glance up every now and then and scatter my vision around.

"Oh Brian, he's okay. Really polite kid. I'd like to see him get his grade up in my class. I know he has the potential. He's a little lazy."

"I know. He can be inconsistent. If he ever cuts up, just tell him you'll call his dad. He knows I don't play." He gives me a stern look as if to back up the information he just gave me about his discipline.

I am speechless momentarily. A teacher who talks in front of about a hundred kids a day for a living was speechless. I have to come back with something. "Sure, not a problem, I understand. Thanks for being supportive."

We continue to talk briefly. I bite the bullet and stared at him. Good Lord. They have parents like this living out here? Fine is an understatement. He has caramel skin, and these amazing eyes. They change from black to dark brown depending on the way the light hit them. They glimmer like a disco ball when he spoke. His hair is jet black, thick and curly. I was transfixed.

What is most mesmerizing is his presence. He appears cool, laid back, intelligent, professional, reserved and genuinely interested in his son's education. He is the classic definition of a tall dark stranger. He continues to tell me that he was a single dad, and that he also has another son attending the high school. He tells me about Brian's home life. Not everything, but enough for me to get a general understanding of the picture. I promise to look out for Brian and let him know if anything was up. We end the conversation and he leaves my classroom.

I feel like I can breathe again. Besides, these damn pants are cutting off my circulation. I should have never pulled them out of the closet...

"Dawn, you have got to stop calling me late. You know I get up with the birds and crack heads."

It was about 12:30 that night. She was hysterical on the phone; I could barely make out what she was saying.

"Alright, alright. I'm coming over. What the hell happened anyway?"

She paused. "I did it. I fucking went psycho on the cocksucker."

4

No Return

Everyone says there are certain moments that define who you are as a person. Who you will become in life. What you will grow into. That is Spirit giving you a life lesson. I have no problem with that.

What I do have a problem with is the timing. It is always at the craziest times. How about this one? God hands you a series of lessons in like what seems the shortest amount of days. You just bounce back and get an emotional grip from one crisis, and the wind gets knocked out of you again. It feels like you're drowning in life's boxing ring. This absolutely sucks.

I throw on some sweatpants and an old tee shirt and sprinted to Dawn's apartment. The scene is unbelievable.

She is standing in the middle of her living room with tears streaming down. There are blotches on her face. Yet, she was so pale that her skin resembled the eggshell color on the wall. Her hair, a black witchy color, was all over the place. She has on jeans and a green tee. What was that on the tee… something red… blood. In her hand she holds a stubby kitchen knife that had spattered blood. Not a lot of blood, but enough to be worried.

"Dawn, what the hell is going on? Are you okay?" I ask in a hushed tone.

"I just lost it." The tears begin coming down again.

"Tell me everything. Now!" I demand.

When you are in a situation like this, a million things go through your mind. *Should I call the cops…is she hurt…did she hurt someone else…did she kill someone?* And with Dawn, that could be anyone. In her fifty five years on earth she had a lot of enemies, visible and invisible.

She has been divorced for about three years. Prior to that, the last twenty one were spent being a housewife to her bitch of an ex husband. He left her for some hoochie he met at work. Dawn gave heart and soul to him and her son, who had since moved away from the Cape after graduating

from college. The divorce situation was and is still a tumul-
tuous one. To add salt to the wound, the hoochie was the
epitome of trailer trash- from the rooter to the tooter. Its one
thing when your man leaves you for someone better: someone with bigger boobs, a bigger ass, or a bigger bank account. To leave you for a sewer rat just puts a woman's
head in a whole different place. I guess this time he pushed
her too far. Mr. Ex had not been paying his alimony on time.
She found out this afternoon when she called to check her
bank account. It was short about a thousand dollars. Then
she called Massachusetts Department of Revenue. They told
her that they had not received any payments from him in
about a month. In turn, this meant they had nothing to
directly deposit in her checking account as a result.

Now, the usual Dawn behavior would have called him
up and cussed him out. But Dawn was in drama mode, and
as Emeril says, she "kicked it up a notch." She was already
pissed over getting fired. This little episode just added fuel
to the fire.

At about 9:30 this evening, after having a few drinks,
Dawn drove over to Mr. Ex's house and snuck in since no
one was home. I guess on one of her many stakeout mis-

sions she knew where they kept the spare key. So after entering the house unauthorized, the vandalizing began. She proceeded to cut up his clothes, along with a few of his new wife's. About midway through her tirade, Mr. Ex came home. An altercation occurred, in which she assaulted Mr.Ex with a small knife. She always kept a knife on her for protection. When she was done, he had a few light flesh wounds on his lower chest and in his arm. I told you before the elevator doesn't quite go to the top floor with her.

"What are you going to do? If you want to turn yourself in, I'll go with you." I am shocked but trying to comfort her at the same time. She stared at me. From her look I knew that option wasn't even on the radar. Whatever her decision, I'm not going to try to change her mind.

She speaks softer. Her hysterics were subsiding. "I just need to get rid of the knife and the tee shirt. I need you to help me. I'm in no shape to drive." I stare at her dimly lit crappy antique lamp in the corner. Scenarios ran through my head.

I grab my keys off her coffee table and stand up. "Let's roll."

5

Crushing

rushing on the parent of one of your students is not good. But crushing on Evan Warner I was. Fiercely crushing.

With everything that happened a few nights ago, I really didn't have time to access the whole date the parent of a student situation. I just put it out of my head. It was never going to work. He was way out of my league. Somebody that hot and put together had to have an entire harem of women stashed away in a secret cave somewhere, like superheroes who always have a secret lair where they keep their gadgets and stuff. Besides, I am his son's teacher. While I don't have a problem with it, I'm sure he would. He seems a little reserved and conservative. To him, going out on a date with his son's social studies teacher would upset an applecart in the universe. I can tell that about him. Alas, this is another cruel joke by God. Dangling a hint of dreaminess in my path that is unattainable is just not fair.

Somehow the little engine that could inside of me wouldn't totally dismiss the idea. I decide to put it on the backburner for a little while.

Yes I covered up Dawn's incident. I am still waiting for the knock at the door in the middle of the night. My students would read about me in the local newspaper court report. I could see it now. Dawn Joanne Mullen would be charged with assault and concealing a crime. I, Kara Mirabelle Campbell, would be charged as an accomplice because I helped hide the weapon. My parents would faint from embarrassment. However, I don't think Mr.Ex will be pressing any charges. Dawn has some dirt on him, and he can't afford the exposure. Truth be told, I really don't give a sweet rat's ass.

I was in full mental capacity when I agreed to help her. How could I turn her down? As dysfunctional as she is, she does deserve some grace. Don't we all? I connect with her. I don't know what it's like to devote yourself to someone for twenty one years. I do know what is like to mourn the death of a relationship. Recently, I ended my own relationship with someone a couple of months before. He mumbled something about "needing space." Prick. After the honeymoon period was over and the reality that both parties involved have to work to maintain a positive relationship settled in, he cut and ran. Lots of men do. That's what separates the men from the boys. It's not the first two months of a relationship that determine the long term potential. It's the period immediately after. I always say the first sixty days are probation anyway. The real man doesn't show up, his representative does. Think of a job interview. You put your best foot forward, smile and tell the prospective employers whatever they want to hear. You do whatever is necessary to get hired. Immediately after you are, boy oh boy, are you on your best behavior. No long lunches, staying late, and promptly returning phone calls. After a few months it's a different story.

What I can identify with is the pain. Men go through pain when their heart is broken, but not like women. Not like women at all. The wave of emotions scales from feeling like open heart surgery without anesthesia to a dull throbbing headache pain. Then there is what I call The Great Depression. The hopelessness. The hallowed shell of a soul left after another has blown in, fucked up your life and blown out. What pisses me off is after it's over, is that you are completely distraught for weeks or months on end and the other person just moves on. Although, I suspect it's a ruse. Over the course of millions of years men have mastered the art of disguising their emotions extremely well.

Thus I found myself in my Nissan Pathfinder driving her through winding beach roads to dispose the evidence of the truth of Dawn's crime. Let's not call it a crime. Let's call it accelerated karma. After all Dawn had been through I don't think it's fair that she has to go down for this. She had a hard life and never received many advantages. I don't trust the universe to administer justice to Mr.Ex. She had to take it into her own hands. She could be waiting forever for the angels to get the order right. Matter of fact, I don't trust the universe to do much of anything anymore, not after the crap I had been through.

We pulled over by Woods Hole harbor and she drops the knife and tee, enclosed in a plastic bag that had seen better days, ceremoniously into the Atlantic Ocean.

Like I said, sometimes you just can't trust the universe…

Enough of that. Let's discuss yesterday's drama, my biopsy for cervical cancer. I guess the best way to describe it would be like this: not exactly hell, but the exit before. For thirty minutes, I was poked and prodded by several not so nice instruments. It felt like a Brillo pad scrubbing away at the last little bit of food on a pan. Then to top it off, they douse you with vinegar to make sure they get a "clean read" down there. Ouch. My parents drove up from Connecticut to come to the appointment with me. As soon as I walked out of the room I informed my mother that it wasn't a pleasant experience. She had decided to wait for me in the doctor's office. My dad was going to wait to, until he freaked out. He took one step in the gynecologist's office after parking the car and look around at the women, including mom and I.

"Nope, I can't do this. I'm going to Home Depot. Call me when you're done."

My mother and I fell out laughing. What is it about men and the gynecologist office? Here's my father, a 200-pound intelligent black man with a top administrative job in a school district. He has a lot of power and yet he is completely thrown off kilter by a few women trying to get their health issues in check. At times my dad could be comedy at its finest.

I was informed that my biopsy results would be returned in about two weeks. More waiting. More not knowing. More crappy comedies to watch.

6

Home Again

"Yo, it's me. Come outside and check out my new whip." I stepped outside to see Brittany in her shiny new Mustang convertible. It's black, a tight new ride alright.

I am so happy she was home. She had returned from what seemed like a million years. She had accepted a job offer halfway across country, but found out after a couple of months that it wasn't exactly what she had hoped for. Brittany and I were like yin and yang. When she left, my yang went crazy. Now she was back, taking some time out to figure out her next move.

I hopped in the passenger seat and she speeds off. "Brit, this is hot." I said.

"I know, before I left California I decided to treat myself. I figured something good had to come out of that crappy experience. So, I bought a new car."

I nod. Brittany and I are the best of friends. Looking at us, you wouldn't think that was so. She is white, petite, with long dark hair and about seven years younger than I. Again, I was Reese cup color, with a short red haircut, with the attitude of a mixture of girl next door meets girl from the hood. Still we melded. We went to one of our local favorite hangouts to grab some food. As we were sitting, we caught up on each other's lives. I decide to bite the bullet and tell her about Evan the hot parent and Dawn's fiasco. The great thing is that Brittany doesn't judge, you can tell her anything. Spilling a secret to her was the equivalent of passing classified information to a CIA agent. In fact she is the only one I trust to talk to about my involvement with Dawn's incident.

Dawn and I have not spoken of the "incident" since it occurred. We made a pact that it happened, and that was it. There would be no need to rehash any of the details in the future. She was forever indebted to me. I knew in her bipolar way she will be there for me when I need her to. There isn't anything else to it.

"Well," she looked at me with her big hazel eyes, "You did what you had to do. I don't fault you for that. That's the problem with people. People are so quick to chastise. But the truth is they don't know what they would have done in the same circumstance." She took a sip of her lemon water. She was forever drinking that damn lemon water.

"How's the depression?" she asked.

"One pill at a time." I said. She nodded and added, "Girl, I feel you."

…The rest of the week sucked. The first grade quarter of the year was closing soon, and I cringed when I saw the averages of some of my students. Many freshmen had tremendous difficulty adjusting first quarter from middle school. Their social studies grade reflects it.

I scan down the list of my World History class. Hmmm. It seems as though young Brian Warner isn't doing so well. Do I dare call his dad Evan to let him know? It's the end of the day. I could go by the office, get his number from a secretary and make contact. What the hell, after all this was about his son, right? Not him. At least I can delude myself.

I stop by one of the many offices in my school grab the number from a secretary and find the nearest empty conference room. I dial Evan's cell number. I'm as nervous as a hooker in church on Easter Sunday as I wait for him to pick up. *Oh good 3 rings, maybe I'll get off by leaving a message.* No such luck.

"Hello?" a deep voice answers.

"Hello, Mr. Warner?" I all but choke out. "This is Ms.Campbell, your son Brian's social studies teacher." I was trying to sound professional but it wasn't working.

"Oh hi, what's up?" he asks.

"I'm calling about Brian. I just checked his average and he's not doing so well. He has a few homework assignments to make up. Also, he has a test this week and I'd like for him to stay after school with me to study."

"Oh, he will, believe it. I will make sure he gets those assignments done tonight and he'll stay after tomorrow. As a matter of fact, let me give you my email address so you can keep me informed of any upcoming assignments or tests."

I quickly jot down his email address. We exchange more pleasantries and end our conversation. Not only is he gorgeous in person but also gracious and very supportive of teachers. Like I said, I'm crushing hard.

As I lay my head on my pillow Sunday night, I actually allow myself to dream. Could I actually have hope that I might have a better life than this? Perhaps if I apply myself a little more to my own goals and give myself permission to be happy every once in a while then I could accomplish something and have a sense of satisfaction. Then the right side of my brain kicked in. *Yeah, yeah, yeah. Whatever.*

7

Action and Inaction

She is back. The lady in the brown dress. Truth is she never really went away. I just tried to ignore her a little. I'm in the car, and poof there she is sitting beside me. I'm at home washing dishes, and I glance across the kitchen. There she is, chilling in a chair. "Shh…soon you will understand."

Could she give me a few more clues than that? In case you haven't guessed, I'm psychic. I see spirits. Or rather they see me and decide to hang out for awhile and have a conversation. This has been going on for the past year. It's a little gift my grandmother bequeathed to me. It's my family heirloom. The people who come to visit most of the time are pretty cool. They usually have a message or two for me or someone around me. I try to decipher them as best I can, but they can get confusing at moments. Things are really different on the other side.

Brown-dress lady keeps saying I'll understand something. Well the only thing I understand is that my life is pretty fucked up right now and nothing is moving in the right direction. For every good thing that occurs, something bad occurs to even it out. This is where the deciphering comes in. If the message doesn't have to do with you, it has to do with someone around you. Hence the game starts. You have to eliminate all possibilities until you narrow it down to one or two suspects. For me that also include nearly 100 students I teach everyday. *Big fun.* And spirits can be pesky little people. They won't say leave you alone until you've done what they need you to do. I am going have to keep my eyes wide open for a bit to figure this out.

My mind kept rotating Evan the "hot parent" like an overcooked pancake. That's it. I'm gonna end this and email him. I decide to make up some bullshit excuse to get in contact with him. Again: anything to delude myself. Time to put this baby to bed. I dig in my schoolbag and retrieve

Evan's email address. Sitting at my computer I take a deep sigh. What the hell was I about to do?

Hi Evan-

I just wanted to let you know I corrected Brian's test and he got an A! I'm proud of him. I know he has the potential to do very well in my class. I'll keep you in the loop. Also, I usually don't do this but would you like have coffee sometime? I don't know very many people out here and it seems we could have some things in common.

Blessings-

Kara Campbell

My heart is fluttering. I closed my eyes and clicked the send button. It's a done deal.

A couple of days later I checked my mail. At the top of the column I see it. IT. The response. I click on the open button.

Hi-

That's great! I am glad that Brian did well on his test. I will be sure to stay involved so that he can get that A that I know he is capable of. Sure, it would be great for us to get together. My cell is 508-555-

2321. I have been busy lately, but I am sure we can find the time to hang out.

 Take care

 Evan

I am ecstatic. There is a role reversal: I had now become the schoolgirl swooning over the high school jock like so many of my students. I quickly email him back and tell him I'll call him later that evening. Perhaps today won't turn out to be such a bad day after all.

Anyone who has chosen education as a career can identify with me when I say that week prior to a school vacation is a dangerous time for teachers and students. No one feels like being around each other: everybody is just getting on everybody's nerves. T High was no different. My students had all but pushed me to the edge and the crazy Black woman inside of me was itching to break loose. I throw a few kids out of class, not for anything serious, just for talking constantly. They wouldn't shut up. It's like they are competing to be the next Oprah Winfrey. Thank God Thanksgiving was only a few days away...

About 9:00 that evening, I nervously dial Evan's number. He picks up on the second ring. What transpires is one of the most enjoyable conversations I have ever had with a member of the other sex. We discuss everything, from Brian and his brother's funny antics to past relationships, philosophies and worldly quagmires. I also learned that he had a young daughter who lived elsewhere. We make plans to get together for coffee the following night.

I am on pins and needles the entire next day. It seems like 2 p.m. can't get here fast enough. I go home and watched *Spongebob Squarepants* the entire afternoon. When I asked Dawn's advice on what to wear yesterday she told me to look sexy and dress provocative. Hel-lo, what kind of message is that going to send? Hi, I'm your son's teacher and also the biggest hoochie on Cape Cod? Instead, I choose some fitting jeans, a tunic top, and my fur boots. I wear a pink pendant around my neck. I am having a good hair day so no need to worry about that. My makeup is visible but understated. I want to look classy but show I have a little kick, too.

We decided to meet at a small local coffeehouse at 8 p.m. I arrive on time and walked in. Scanning the room nervously, I see he isn't there. Good, I have a few more minutes to collect myself. I wait in line at the counter to order a chai tea and began to pour a tremendous amount of sugar in it. I don't know why I have to have like 10 teaspoons of sugar in my tea all the time, I thought to myself.

"Did I tell you I'm always late?" a voice says behind me, as I pour sugar into my tea.

"Oh, that's okay, it's no big deal." I smile, trying to break the ice. Aah, those eyes. I could get lost in them for awhile. He was wearing jeans, Timberland boots, a striped shirt, and a sweater. I am convinced he has a nice shirt fetish. Twice I've seen him and he's worn really nice crisp starched shirts. Just like my Hitler-esque psychiatrist's obsession with hair. It's amazing what we women notice about men: the oddest things. I carry my tea to an open table and waited for him.

He arrived shortly thereafter, latte in hand. Don't you hate first dates? Was this even a date or two people hanging out? Many thoughts ran through my mind. Does he think I'm attractive? Will I be witty enough? Was I going to spill something all over myself, the table, or both? However things went very smoothly. We have a lot in common. He tells me so many funny stories about his kids I don't think

I'll ever look at Brian or his brother, Brandon, the same again. I can tell his children really did light up his life.

The next morning, I awake to the ringing of my cell phone. It's my dad.

He wants to know when I was coming home for Thanksgiving. I tell him not soon enough. The way my students were acting, there was going to be a homicide if I don't get the hell out of here.

8

Meet the Campbells

Going home for the holidays is a little like gambling. I just never knew what hand I was going to be dealt in terms of what relatives were showing up. Some trips I got off easy, and burned a white candle the minute I returned that I survived. Other trips I had to pack extra antidepressants and stay all but completely inebriated to survive. It was never my immediate family: just the extra characters that showed up.

I hail from New Haven, Connecticut. It's a bustling city primarily due to the fact it is home to Yale University. I measure my travel time by the amount of CDs I can listen to. From the Cape to New Haven it's about 3 and a half CDs. I pull into the luxury condominiums estate where they live. It's the day before Thanksgiving. I always try to time my visits perfectly: show up the day before endure the pain the day of, and roll out soon thereafter. As I turned into our driveway I breathe a short sigh of relief. No other cars are present beside my parent's and sister's.

"Hey Baby!" My mom says as she opens the door. She is the only woman I know who still maintained a southern accent after transplanting herself in the north over 30 years ago. My dad doesn't have his anymore. Mom, otherwise known to the world as Klara Campbell is an attractive, intelligent, and hip 50ish woman. She wears one of those chic bobs that you see in the hair commercials. I see she had dyed it a different color since I saw her last time. Both of my parents are overachievers. They worked very hard through stressful times to achieve success. After earning her doctorate degree over 10 years ago, my mom accepted a full time professorship teaching psychology at one of our local colleges. My dad currently serves as Assistant Superintendent to the town adjacent to ours. My sister Liz comes out of the kitchen and gives me a big hug. I am the oldest and she's the baby. We look just alike except she has long hair. We are daddy's little girls. Liz fills me in on how her graduate program was going as well as some sorority business. We all belong to Alpha Kappa Alpha Sorority. The phone rings. It was Aunt IT confirming dinner time for the next day.

That's right. I said Aunt IT. She is my mom's sister. My mom hates when my sister and I refer to her with this name. She is undoubtedly one of the most miserable women on this earth. I mean if I am pissed off at the world about 70 percent of the time, then Aunt IT is pissed off 100 percent. She is pure evil.

How my grandmother bore both my mother and her out of the same body is a mystery. They are just so radically different. Physically, Aunt IT resembled a big-boned, dark-skinned linebacker. She had been beaten by the ugly stick at birth. No let me rephrase- she had been pummeled by the ugly stick at birth. She is the oldest sister, in her early sixties. She had been divorced a couple of times. I didn't blame the men. Who would want to wake up to that every morning? The only gift the universe had given the rest of her family is that she hadn't procreated. I shudder to think what that baby would have looked like. I tried to imagine a couple of times, but my mind just blocked it out. I think it's too traumatic. It was like one of those emotional blackouts my psychiatrist is always talking to me about.

So, Aunt IT was coming to dinner for Thanksgiving at about 3 pm. I glance in the den just to make sure the bar is well stocked. We are going to need as much help as we could get.

Thanksgiving morning was the usual family flurry of activity. My mother informed me half way through breakfast of more guests attending.

"Set four extra places, because your dad's stepsister is coming with her family." she says.

This is going to be comedy. Coretta Campbell is my father's estranged stepsister. She and her husband are one of the sweetest couples I know. She gets along very well with us, we just have sporadic contact with her because her husband is in the Navy and they relocate often. Right now they are stationed in Rhode Island and decided to drive down for the day.

Here's where life gets a little tricky. Corretta and her husband Tim have a set of twin boys, Darryl and Dougie. They are about 10 years old now. Both have Tourette's Syndrome. If you are not familiar with this, let me give you the quick and dirty version. At times, they will exhibit tics or uncontrollably blurt out words, usually swear words. I have never seen Aunt IT and Darryl and Dougie in the same room before. Armageddon is pregnant and pending.

3:00 arrives with the speed of tax season and everything is in place. Aunt IT arrived first with poison lips in hand. Corretta, Tim and the boys come shortly thereafter.

"What the hell is the matter with those kids?" Aunt IT asked my mother in the kitchen. "Why do they keep twitching and shit?"

"They have Tourette's." My mother quickly explains the scenario.

"Well thank god your kids didn't get that gene. I told you Dave didn't have good genes in his family. You have to be careful who you sleep with. Every X and Y chromosome don't always line up you know." So now Aunt IT is a doctor. She often went off on tangents about how my father wasn't good enough for my mother. We just ignore her. Secretly I believe she's just bitter that she was alone and jealous that my parents had been happily married for 35 years.

Dinner is awesome- until dessert. Apparently, Darryl and Dougie had switched meds recently and their bodies were having trouble adjusting. The swearing begins.

"She is a--- fat ass."

It flew threw the air and shattered the good holiday mood.

That's how it often happened. Darryl would begin and Dougie would finish the line. It was typical twin nature to finish each other's thoughts. They just do it out loud. Aunt IT glares at Coretta as she tries to apologize for her sons' behavior and chastise them at the same time. I am surprised Aunt IT doesn't throw the dessert coffee in her face immediately.

"I don't believe in all of this doctor shit, you need to give your kids an old fashioned ass whipping. You guys are really sorry parents."

"I'll thank you not to school me on how to raise my children." I am waiting for Tim to come to his wife's rescue and chime in, but he declined. He could be such a pushover at times. My mother quickly tried to change the conversation but it's too late. They are already at the impasse. The argument continues. It is old school versus new school.

Aunt IT is not about to be upstaged by some thirtyish attractive woman, even if she is family. She's very competitive. This competitiveness didn't carry over into any other areas of her life so this is her only 15 minutes of fame. Family gatherings were the only place where she could feel like a queen because the rest of her life sucked. The twins, sensing their mother is losing the battle, stepped in where their father didn't.

"Fuck----you."

"Bitch Ass----Whore."

"You need a man---- sorry motherfucker."

I get up and grab another glass of red wine, settling down and strapping in for the next round. Out of the mouths of babes.....

9

Apathy and Hope

January 22. I can't believe half of the school year has passed. About the only thing I am thankful for at the end of the year is that my biopsy results were negative.

Actually, I have been feeling really crappy lately. Another year has passed. None of my goals have been accomplished. I am just hanging on going through the motions like most working drones. I didn't buy a house or start my part-time business. It's my ultimate dream to design clothes and sell them online. So much for that. What's holding me back is total fear. I'll admit it. Sometimes it paralyzes me. Fear of falling flat on my face once again. I have attempted the business thing a few times but with very limited success. If I thought about it realistically, I know I could do it. Start off slowly, be consistent and watch it grow. But I'm very impatient and critical. In the past, as soon as I didn't get the results I expected, I bailed. Bailed, beat up myself, and cried.

I have been thinking a lot about love the past few days. I had spoken to Evan a few more times via phone, but he had not made any suggestion about us getting together again. When I suggested it he acted interested but something would fall through. Yet, we would have these three hour phone conversations. So if he isn't interested in me, then why would he spend all this time conversing with me? I'm bewildered by his behavior. He seems attracted to me and yet he pulls away. I think it goes beyond the teacher thing, too. I can't put my finger on it. Sometimes I feel he is trying to be my friend and keep me on the hook a little while he figures out his next move. When we talked he made it clear that he is extremely single. But a girl knows. He had to be getting maintenance sex from somewhere. I'm not stupid. And is it really my business-no. Furthermore, from what I could discern from our conversations, there may be several exes in the picture.

Men often don't see women clearly. My senses told me that his exes were like circling sharks, waiting for the day that he would choose to be with one of them. They may have been playing the *Oh we'll be friends* role or *I'll always be there for your kids,* but I knew different. His kids are loveable, but those exes wouldn't be doing that unless something was in it for them. It simply wasn't out of the kindness of their heart. Women can be very manipulative when they want to. And why not- he is gorgeous. To them he would always be the one that got away. In addition to that, I knew he has a couple of friends "with benefits." I'm not saying he's the type who gets around. I'm just saying that my senses picked up that the player inside him hadn't quite died yet.

Do I really want to be in the Evan Warner race? Do I want to do the work? He seems like a hell of a lot of work. He has kids, exes, women constantly after him, and a vicious schedule he adheres to like glue. I am beginning to feel that I want to surrender my membership card to his fan club. Perhaps we would make better friends. Maybe that's all he wants in me and I'm jumping the gun. But yet at times I feel this strange connection to him I can't explain.

It's like we have a shot, but the timing just isn't quite right in our lives now. Regardless, my intuition tells me that I definitely need to chill and lay low for a little while. He needs to be placed on the backburner. Besides, I am sure he has um- other females to keep him occupied...

The Great Depression sunk in again about a week ago. The trigger was me registering about 6 pounds heavier on the scale one morning. I need to do something about that. I don't want to be on the beach this summer and someone look at me and yell "It's a manatee!"

I mean there just has to be more to life than this. Working and paying bills and occasionally having fun to me did not constitute a quality life. I feel stymied. Stuck. I'm close to the edge.

Later that week an annoying parent of one of my students called my department head. She wanted to schedule a meeting because she felt that I was singling her son out when I graded him. I had been battling this parent all year. Her name was "Mrs. Streinsborg." That's just an alias. Her real name is female Dracula. Remember when I told you about the type of parents who believe all teachers are the devil and want to fail kids? She falls into that category. She questions every little grade or discipline write up I submitted to his dean. Now she had contacted my department head because she didn't understand why Jamie was failing. How about the fact that he submitted 5 out of 27 homework assignments? Hmm... or could it be that he had a test average of 37.3? Of course, this is completely my fault. This is the growing trend in education-blame the teacher and the school because I'm not doing my job at home and don't want to feel guilty about it.

The meeting is tense. I had built up so much anger inside of me that it's quite difficult to maintain a professional appearance. My boss mediates. She was very familiar with the situation and had my back. However, to pacify female Dracula, she asks me to send home a weekly email to her. *Oh great.* Let's just make more work for the teacher. Whatever. I feel like I'm being professionally attacked. These meetings can be very emotionally draining. I drive home a limp ball of nerves, right by the gym-literally. I had pledged to myself to do better about getting there. But not today.

I crashed and awake about 3 hours later. There's a surprise when I checked my messages on my cell phone.

"What's up Kara, its Evan. What are you up to this weekend? I was wondering if we could get together. There's something I need some advice on. Call me when you get this."

I wonder what that could be about. I know it can't be about Brian because he would have just emailed me. I scramble to dial his number in the half dark. We speak quickly because he's on the way to visit a friend.

Tomorrow. 7:30. Drinks.

I can barely withhold my anticipation.

10

Friends?

After this week, nothing could be sweeter than being able to meet Evan for drinks. I can't wait to drown my sorrows into a few Midori Sours and look into his glimmering eyes. We decide to meet at a local restaurant. It is small and quaint. I like that because sometimes in bars you really can't hear what the other person is saying. This place is different.

Evan is a few minutes late, fulfilling his self- proclaimed prophecy. I had already grabbed a table for us. He strode in with that usual sexy swagger. He was impeccably dressed in a hip hop meets business casual manner. After exchanging pleasantries, we ordered our drinks.

"What's going on? You said you wanted to run something by me. Is Brian okay?" I sip a little anxiously.

"Yeah, he's cool. He talks about your class all the time. He likes you a lot."

"I must admit he is one of my favorites. We are very close. I'm hard on him and I think he respects that."

"Thanks for looking out for him for me. Anyhow, I need some advice on something." He sighs. Then, he drops the bomb.

"My daughter's mom and I have been talking about getting back together."

I blinked. It is a *Twilight Zone* moment.

So much for being in the Evan Warner race. I am not even in the running. Shit. I am in the friend danger zone. If you have ever wanted to date a friend, you know this zone. You are just a confidant- never looked at as a potential partner. His statement clarified any confusion I had about us. I have to play this off well.

"Is this what you want?" I ask. My composure never wavered.

He stares at the floor and looks up sheepishly.

"I don't know."

"We have such a crazy history together. I want to be able to see my daughter whenever and if she and I are back together then it won't be such a big deal."

"I'm feelin ya on that. But do you still love her? I know you said that you two had mad drama. I know it's hard to cut ties with an ex, but I can't imagine how you feel. I don't have a child. And to be fair, I don't really know this woman. What I am saying is, are you going back to her out of guilt? What good is it for you two to be together if you are going to fight all the time? That's not going to help your little one."

He stares at me intently for what seemed like an eternity and lets it all sink in. I'm playing devil's advocate hard core. He is an extremely intelligent man. I am just waiting for him to rip me to shreds. But he doesn't.

"Believe me. I have thought about all of this. I just don't know. I love my daughter to pieces and I want to be with her as much as I can. If we get back together then maybe she'll move back here and they can live with me. How do you think Brian and Brandon will take all of this?"

Well that is a loaded question.

"Listen, all I can say is don't rush into anything. If you are thinking about getting serious with her again, then take it slow. Let it ride for a couple of months. See if she's going to put you through the same manipulative crap she did before. If not, then discuss her relocating. But I would tell the boys what's going on every step of the way and include their opinion in your decision. It's going to be a major change for all three of you. It's going to impact them on a daily basis. And while I am sure they will love having their little sister around, they may not feel the same about her. I don't have a 100% positive feeling about this. Have you talked to your mom and your friends? What do they say?"

He nods and adds, "They told me to think things through and not to make any quick decisions. I just wanted to run this by you because I trust you. You're really good at picking up on people and situations."

Just call it my psychic "spidey" sense, Evan. Of course I couldn't tell him that.

I feel like a lawyer saying my closing argument in front of a jury.

"Listen Evan, I haven't known you that long, but you are a great guy. You really got it going on. Any woman would be proud to have you as her man. Just be sure that she's not using your feelings about your daughter to catch you as the brass ring. Make sure that if you do decide to settle down with whomever, you do it because you absolutely know they love you for you. All of you. The good. The bad. The obsessive compulsive cleaner in you." He laughed. It's a joke between us that he's extremely OCD.

"Don't make the mistake of thinking that you have to exchange your happiness in love for your daughter's love. You can have both. You deserve both." He smiles.

It was done. I said it. Case closed.

"Thanks. It's a miracle someone hasn't snatched you up yourself yet." He adds. It catches me off guard.

I wave my right hand in protest. "Don't even go there. I've got too much to do. Besides, who the hell wants to put up with my crazy ass anyway?" I laugh.

He smiles again. "Another round?"

"Absolutely." I say enthusiastically. Anything to keep looking into those glimmering eyes. He is such a sexy motherfucker.

11

Supermaxx Freakout

"Dawn!" I rap on the door fanatically. I'm tipsy and already buzzing from the three drinks I had at the restaurant with Evan. She opens the door.

"Now who is harassing who?" she chides. "What's up?"

"I HATE EVAN WARNER!" I yell.

"Oh Lord, Kara what happened? You better come in here and stop screaming outside."

I come in and sat in a chair. She had been watching re-runs of *Murder, She Wrote*. The empty DVD case is on the top of her bookcase. *Hey, that's one of my favorite shows.* She always told me she hated it. I fill her in on my evening.

"That's totally fucked up. You really don't hate him, you're just disappointed. And rightfully so. Maybe he did indirectly lead you into thinking you guys could have something more. Want me to stab him for ya?"

"What the hell- oh. No. I don't need to be an accessory to another crime. I'm good."

"Well in that case- how about a margarita? I just mixed up a pitcher for myself."

"Sure, it's not like I have to drive anywhere."

"Just be careful not to trip over anything when you go home. You can always crash on the couch if the ten feet between your apartment and mine are too much."

I know I am going to regret this in the morning. I can already feel the post inebriation hangover kicking in. But what the fuck. I am bitter and tired of being the fucking nice girl next door. I should have just laid my cards on the table when Evan brought up the conversation about reconciling with his ex. I should have told him how I truly felt about him and been more direct. But I took the high road. I am pissed at myself for it.

I awake sometime the next afternoon. I still don't feel good emotionally. I feel as if everything is falling in on me. I throw on my favorite AKA sorority sweat suit and decide to run a couple of errands.

Supermaxx was the type of store in my town that carries everything. I mean everything. For the most part, the prices were fairly cheap. I just like to go to people watch. People of all shapes and sizes and kinds frequent there. I only need a few items. It shouldn't take long, I told myself. Besides I still have a headache from my pity party the night before. I grab a cart and get my stuff. I find a checkout line. It was relatively long, but usually this store was good about swift service.

I wait. And wait. And wait. The cashier runs out of quarters and we have to wait for someone to replenish her supply. Then there are two price checks. Then about three people have coupons. One of the coupons isn't ringing up correctly, so the floor manager has to come over and intervene. My patience is being tested to the utmost. I glanced around but all of the other lines are just as long, so there's no use in my vacating.

I'm now starting to feel on edge. I had forgotten in my rush to take my daily antidepressants. Aunt Flo had come to visit a couple of days before and I could feel the next wave of cramps coming. One person is ahead of me. I need to checkout and get to my car quick. I have extra pain relievers and antidepressants in my glove compartment for times like these. Then fate intervenes.

As soon as I begin putting my items on the conveyer belt, the bitch has the nerve to put up her closed sign.

"Sorry, I'm on break."

"You know, I've been waiting a really long time and I don't feel so well. Could you just check me out?" I say in a humble manner.

Then the bitch comes out in her.

She looks at me scornfully and says with a nasty tone, "No, I'm going on break. Don't you see the sign? Are you blind? Get in the line next to this one." She is obviously one of those employees who thinks her title is more than her sorry ass position. I start trippin.

Oh hell no. Hell hath no fury like the wrath of a crazy black woman who hasn't taken her meds. I flip on the bitch.

"You know what bitch? If you don't wait on me, some-one else will RIGHT NOW. I don't have time for this shit. You had me and all of these other people waiting in this mad long line forever and you think that you can speak to me any old way because you are due for a sorry ass fifteen minute break? I'll tell you what. Fuck You. Get me the fucking manager now. I am not leaving this line until I pay for my shit."

She looks at me stunned. I guess she could dish out the nastiness but is surprised when it is returned. The people behind me in the line stare blankly, especially the White people. I hear one of them whisper "Oh I can't believe she said that." I don't know if they are in awe or fear. I really don't give a sweet rat's ass.

She regains her composure and calls for the floor manager on the phone. She's obviously shaken. I could tell because she keeps playing with one of the ties on her red Supermaxx smock. The manager comes over quickly. I explain to her what happened matter of factly.

"Maam, I'm really sorry about that. Let's get you checked out so that you can feel better."

Finally! Some fucking results. I pay for my shit. I feel liberated. I know the emotional storm is coming and going to unfurl at any moment. I'm not surprised. That's how it happens. The crazy Black woman inside of me doesn't show up often. She leaps out just when I need her to. Just when I've had enough of all of the bullshit.

And boy oh boy had I had enough. The bad ass students. The pain in the ass parents. Grades. The never quite achieving my goals. The cancer scare. The Aunt Its in the world. Even the crime cover up. Then, meeting a wonderful guy who I can never have because he's still in love with his crazy ex and there are so many obstacles between us that it will just never work and oh my god why does this always happen to me, I just want to be happy in love. The constantly being a martyr and not getting a break from the universe. There, it's said. All in one breath- in my thoughts. Venting done.

12

Under

I get through my apartment door and start crying. I don't know why. It's like a faucet that I can't turn off. I want to be numb for awhile and not think about all of this shit.

I take a few more pain relievers and antidepressants and add in a couple of sleeping pills. I really don't remember how many. I decide to chase it down with a few glasses of white wine so that I can have a solid comatose sleep. It's Saturday afternoon and it isn't like my dance card is full for the evening.

A few hours later, I think somewhere around 10:30, I repeated the process. More pain relievers, more antidepressants, more sleeping pills, more wine.

All I can remember is waking up in a hospital room.

Dawn and Brittany tell me that sometime Sunday afternoon, I knocked on Dawn's door and tell her that I'm not feeling well. I make it to her couch and collapse. She can't wake me up, so she calls 911. Upon arrival at the hospital, she flips through my cell, finds Brittany and my parent's numbers and contact them. My parents are en route.

When the doctor enters the room, Dawn and Brittany leave. She says her name is Dr.Pinnella. I do recall she is a very pretty Hispanic woman. She tells me that I had over-medicated myself and they had to pump my stomach. She asked me if I had a history of depression. I respond with a resounding yes. She then asks me if I meant to do this on purpose, you know, to end it. I tell her no, I just wanted to sleep for awhile because I was really stressed out. Or maybe I did want to end it and am just deluding myself. Yeah, I guess I wanted to end it.

When my parents arrive, I guess Dr.Pinnella fills them in on what had happened. They tell her that I had struggled with depression since my teenage years and this was not the first time I tried to hurt myself. She recommends rest and intense therapy. They fill out the paperwork for me to be released in their care until I can check into a facility.

My parents and I discuss everything. My mother cries. I feel bad. She is such a strong woman and it hurts her that I am hurting myself. My father is confused. He thinks I had covered all of this in therapy and does not understand why it is happening again. I tell him therapy sucked and I just wanted a break. I just wanted to breathe and get out of the rat race. He tells me to have faith.

I wanted a break and I got it. God knew I was tired and he delivered rest. My parents called my school. Luckily because I am a teacher, I have more than enough sick days accumulated to take a three week leave of absence. Furthermore it was three weeks prior to our mid-winter school vacation, so I would get an additional week to recuperate. My department head is wonderful. She promises to keep everything confidential and tell inquiring minds that I'm having "elective surgery" and will be out for awhile. She tells me to make my health a priority because I am not good to myself, what good would I be to my students?

I tell her I will email her lesson plans for my classes before I leave for the funny farm.

13

In

Greenwood Retreat is in western Massachusetts, surrounded by the Berkshire Mountains. It is a relatively small facility. There are no more than about 45 people there at any one time. My parents and I selected it after the hospital's recommendation. Actually it's pretty. It's a very old Victorian estate that was renovated about 30 years ago. I like my bedroom. Apparently, some old rich lady who had mental problems all her life left it to some organization in a will. The food isn't too bad either. I am thankful for the small things. I didn't want to end up in some large impersonal place for treatment. This place is fairly laid back. I can come and go as I please, not that there is much to do in this one-horse town. We have small group sessions and individual therapy.

Boy! I thought I was crazy, but some of these people in here are a few french fries short of a happy meal. The center only treats anxiety, bipolar, and depression issues. It seems as though the anxiety people had it the worst. They do some weird shit. Like stare out the window and twitch. Or pace back and forth. I think there is only one simple difference between people with anxiety issues and people with depression issues. If you are anxious, you exhibit your fears about the world to the world. If you are depressed, you exhibit your fears about the world only to yourself. It really didn't matter. Here, we are all assorted nuts in a trail mix you buy at the grocery store.

I am often quiet during the group sessions. I figured I better let everyone else have their fifteen minutes of fame. I listen instead. I can hear their pain. It is the same story rewritten a thousand times, from Marilyn Monroe to the teenager who cuts to bleed out her anguish.

The spirits have been visiting me on a regular basis. It's almost as if they have to take a number to speak with me. I guess in a place where there's so much stress and healing taking place all at once, they can't help but be drawn to the energy. They have many messages to share with their loved ones. Word has gotten out that I am some kind of psychic. I did a reading for my roommate and that opened the floodgates. I can't turn them down. When I found out that I had the "gift", I made a promise to the man upstairs that I would use it to help and heal. For some of these people in here, a kind word from someone from the other side might make the difference as to whether or not I saw them at breakfast the next morning. One lesson I have quickly learned in here: never underestimate the power of a few words of encouragement.

A couple of nights ago, brown dress lady came to see me again.

"Aah, I was wondering where you had been. You disappeared on me." I said to her.

"Soon you will understand." She continued with that message.

"Is this about me or someone else?"

"Oh, make no mistake this is all about you." She was gone. I fell back to sleep as sound as a baby. Somehow I had the knowledge that the time for me to understand was drawing quite near.

I wake up a little late the next morning, and make my way to my individual therapy appointment downstairs.

I am learning a lot. I can honestly say that my mind and my emotions were being opened up and finally healing in the right direction. I like my psychiatrist. Her name is Joyce. She is African American like me and wears her hair in a close cut Afro. It's speckled with gray which speaks volumes about her wisdom before she even opened her mouth. I also admire her because she has the craziest sense of humor I have ever encountered in a medical professional.

Joyce and I get to the heart of many issues during our long talks and today is no different. That's another thing that I liked about this place. There was no clock ticking on your sessions. When you are finished, you are finished. The psychiatrists and therapists only see about four people a day. Today, she decides to explore my relationships with men.

When I was young, I was sexually abused for about 7 years by a distant older cousin. Although this is the source of why I had been in therapy for so long, she put it into perspective for me in a new way. One thing people don't understand about abuse is that you never really get over it. You just find ways to cope with what happened to you.

She tells me that she thinks I have serious trust issues with men. I tell her the only man I really ever trusted is my father. He's the one person that I know will never betray me. He's broken my heart a few times because he's human first. Maybe I didn't get the toy I wanted one Christmas or he should have sided with me instead of my mom in an argument. But he will never betray me.

Joyce says that because of what happened to me I never feel seriously comfortable sharing my feelings with men. I am afraid that they will bail on me. She mentions that the reason that I am having difficulty achieving my goals is because I don't think I deserve them to begin with. That's why as soon as things get hard I abandon ship. It's a self-fulfilling prophecy. When things go south I could say "Oh well, I knew it wasn't meant to be anyway." It is an emotional payoff. This included love, too.

She sipped on her Earl Gray tea.

"You mentioned this Evan guy a couple of sessions ago. Want to talk about it?"

"Why the hell not? I'm up for a challenge." I smirked.

I fill her in. Then I listened to her wisdom.

"Kara, let me tell you about men-especially Black men. Most of them are just as terrified about being abandoned in relationships as we are. They simply hide it better. If you suspect that he has a few part-time relationships going on, then he probably does. You know this. Half of the facility swears about your psychic abilities. And it's okay if he does. Men grow only through experience. That just shows you where he is emotionally right now. We all mature at different rates. You can't and shouldn't fault him for that. I am sure he was hurt deeply in the past and has vowed never to let that happen again. The only way he can do that is by not getting too close. I do think he likes you as more than a friend, though. Don't let him fool you about that. He may talk and act a good game, but he likes you. See through all of the bullshit."

I sit back on the couch and take a sip from my water bottle. I have never let it fully enter my mind that Evan is attracted to me. She continues.

"Listen. Men love attention. I'm sure that's another reason why he won't completely be with one person right now. Why try to work on something real with one person when he can have all of these mini fantasy relationships with different chicks? Men will often delude themselves about their feelings and women. It feeds their ego. By handling them with a long handled spoon, it keeps him in control. It keeps him pulling the strings. He doesn't have to worry about getting hurt. He pulls the strings and they dance. And he gets some ass while he's at it."

I chuckle. It makes sense.

"Evan is not a bad guy. In fact, from what you've told me it sounds as if he is great. So don't give up too easily. You never know. Time reveals all things. We write our future in the present. Be his friend if you feel you can still handle it. Keep your options open. If someone asks you to dinner, accept. Don't put all your eggs in one basket. Perhaps after the smoke has cleared with his other relationships, and you have done some healing yourself, you two might have a shot together. But you can't worry about that. Focus on building positive relationships with men by building a positive relationship with yourself. We teach people how to treat us." She takes another sip of tea.

Speaking with her was like talking with a long lost aunt at a family reunion.

As brown dress lady said, it really was all about me. And I finally understand. More than I ever knew.

14

Out

They let me out of the funny farm. I am both happy and sad when it comes time to go.

Joyce made me promise to visit her at least a couple of times a year and be a guest in her home. I can tell that we will have a lifelong friendship that goes beyond the doctor/client relationship. She tells me to get in contact with her if I ever think about hurting myself again. She will pick me up in a flash.

I am still allowed to be on meds. However, they switched them. I'm also referred to a reputable psychiatrist affiliated with Cape Cod Hospital for weekly appointments. They ask me not to drink alcohol for at least the first four weeks I am home. I designate Brittany and Dawn as my caretakers. They graciously agree. I am supposed to talk to them if I feel I am in trouble and they are to make the necessary arrangements in case anything goes down. However, Joyce feels like I'm strong enough, and this isn't going to happen again. My parents pick me up.

"Wow, you lost some weight. Did they feed you in here?" mom asks.

"Yep, they did. I just worked out a lot because I actually had time to exercise for a change." They actually had a bomb ass gym. I also had started practicing yoga.

My dad gives me a big hug and grabs my bags. My parents stay on the Cape a couple of days to get me readjusted to life on the outside. Dawn and Brittany take me out to a celebration dinner that night. A couple of days later, I was back at Townshend High, ready to teach World War 1.

My department head is pleased to see me and says I looked well rested. In fact all of my co-workers say it. I am anxious to know about how my students had been doing in my absence.

Apparently, not well, according to my boss. It seems that they essentially were in rebellion. They kept complaining that they had the substitute from hell and weren't learning a thing. "When's Ms.Campbell coming back? This sub is wack." That was the general cry. I had missed them too. At times they made me wish I kept a shotgun behind my desk. They could be bad ass students when they wanted to, but they were my bad ass students. Truth is no one really understood them the way I did. I'll admit it. I do have a gift. The school's biggest juvenile delinquents would get A's and B's in my class. Why? Because I listened to them, laugh with them, and let them know I don't take any shit. Kids respect that.

My homecoming and return to work go rather smoothly-except for one hiccup. One big hiccup.

Besides my immediate family and Brittany and Dawn, the only other person that knew what had happened to me was my good friend Adrienne. She was an African American sister who is a dean at my school. She and I had been through mad shit. She is also close friends with Evan. Her husband plays basketball with him in an intramural league. She also knows about the crush I have on him.

I knock on her door after school. She is excited to see me and eager to hear about my experience. Then she lets the cat out of the bag.

Evan stopped by her office after school a few days earlier. He was concerned about Brian, and more specifically-me and my whereabouts. Brian's grades were slipping and he wasn't doing well in social studies at all. He said that he had tried to call me several times to see if I was okay, but I hadn't responded. He was concerned for me as a friend, not only as his son's teacher. He wanted to know when I was coming back.

Adrienne told him everything. Before I could strangle her she told me why. She said that she knew Evan and I were good friends and she felt that I would need as much support as I could when I returned. She told him that I had a crush on him. He was surprised, at least he acted surprised but he didn't say anything. I thank her. I'm not mad at her because I know she did this from the heart. I tell her I hadn't even checked my messages because I just want to ease back into things. I did see his number in my missed call directory but I dismissed it. I'm not ready to deal with him yet.

Besides I am trying to remain positive. My free time has been spent recently playing with my newly adopted kitten, Tiramisu. She's white with brown patches in her fur and absolutely adorable. It feels good to come home to something alive at the end of the day. I'm getting to the gym at least 3 times a week. My mom and dad surprised me recently and told me that after the school year was over, they would help me purchase my first house this summer. They said that perhaps I won't feel so displaced if I have something to call my own. I'm deeply thankful. I have also decided to enroll in an online MBA program in the fall. I only wanted to take one course at a time so that I didn't overload myself. If I am going to own a business and do it right, I need as much knowledge as possible.

I had been staying after school an hour or two late everyday to try to catch up on lecture notes and paperwork. The kids are right. They hadn't learned much. Sometimes, Brian and a couple of other students stay after while waiting for sports practice to begin. They straighten up the desks for me. We laugh and trip. They tell me about the antics that went on while I was away and fill me in on the latest T High gossip.

At about 3:15 one afternoon while I am working, I hear a knock on my classroom door.

"Come in. I'm here." I say nonchalantly. I thought it was a janitor. Matter of fact, I didn't even look up from my laptop.

"Hey stranger. Good to see you back at work."

It is Evan.

15

Next

"**W**hat's up?" I am surprised beyond belief. He is the last person I expected to see standing in my classroom doorway.

"What are you doing here?" I ask.

"I had a couple of meetings with Brandon and Brian's teachers. I'm trying to get them back on track. I wanted to take a chance and pop by to see if you were still here."

"Nice surprise." I say. I'm trying maintaining my professional composure. I hadn't discerned whether the nature of his visit is professional or personal and I don't want to jump to any conclusions. He comes over near me and sits down in an empty desk.

"I just wanted you to know that I'm glad you're back and feeling better. I was a little worried. Did you get my messages?" he asks.

"Yes, I did. It was nothing against you. I didn't want to deal with anyone for awhile. I had to process some things going on in my life. I appreciate you checking on me though. It's thoughtful."

I was trying to remain matter of fact when I answered his questions. He smiled. Then he lowers his head and glances away. I know enough about Evan in our brief face-to-face interactions that when he does this, he's about to say something serious. Like I said before, his eyes always tell his story. When he stops having eye contact with you, something is brewing and he is gathering his thoughts. He looks back up after a few seconds.

"Listen, I need to talk to you about a few things. Do you have a few minutes?"

"Sure. Go ahead and spill it." I already know what the conversation is going to be about but I let him take the lead.

"Adrienne let me know what was going on. I wasn't prying. I was just concerned." he says.

"Yes, she mentioned that to me a couple of days ago. Don't worry: it's not interfering with my ability to teach Brian." I say.

I worry that he thinks I won't be able to effectively teach his son and that he will request he be moved to another class. That would be so embarrassing. But it would be understandable.

"No, no, where did you get that idea? That's not it at all. I'm here as your friend."

"Oh." I say with a sigh of relief.

"Listen, you can always talk to me about anything." he says.

"I don't want any pity. I'm doing okay right now, but thank you anyway." I state in a mildly defensive manner. My guard is up with him. I don't want to be his damsel in distress. He has enough damsels in distress.

"Chill. I'm sincerely here to see how you are doing-not as Brian's teacher, but as a friend. You can relax. There's no ulterior motive with me. Trust me, if I didn't want to be bothered with you, I wouldn't be here."

I am attempting to take this all in at once without showing too much defiance and fragility.

"You are one of the strongest Black women I have ever known and I know you will be fine."

I was deeply touched. The conversation continues.

"You were right about my daughter's mother." he says.

My mind is turning. *Where did that come from…?*

"In a short story, she hasn't changed that much at all. I found out recently that she is seeing someone. She wants to keep me on the hook until she sees which way the ball is going to bounce with her new man. She knows my daughter is my Achilles' heel." He says.

I tell him that I was sorry it happened. Truth is I'm not, but it seems like the appropriate thing to say. He continues…

"I'd like us to get to know each other when you are ready. I know you are going through some stuff right now." he says.

Okay, so how am I supposed to digest this one? There goes the universe again, throwing me another curveball.

"Evan, I truly am flattered. But right now I have a lot of healing to do. Perhaps we can be good friends right now and work on something happening in the future between us?" I say. In addition, I don't want to be the rebound girl, as tempting as the offer is.

"I have a lot of emotional closet cleaning to do myself. My latest fiasco with my daughter's mom is sort of forcing me to refocus my energies. I want to reassess my goals." he says.

We both agree not to jump into anything until we were ready because co-dependent relationships are not cute.

"So, what are you getting into this weekend?" he finally asks.

"Hopefully, a cup of coffee and dessert with you." I reply.

He smiles at me.

"Definitely sounds like a plan." he answers.

One thing I knew for sure, my days as a martyr are definitely over.

Printed in the United States
146040LV00003B/8/P